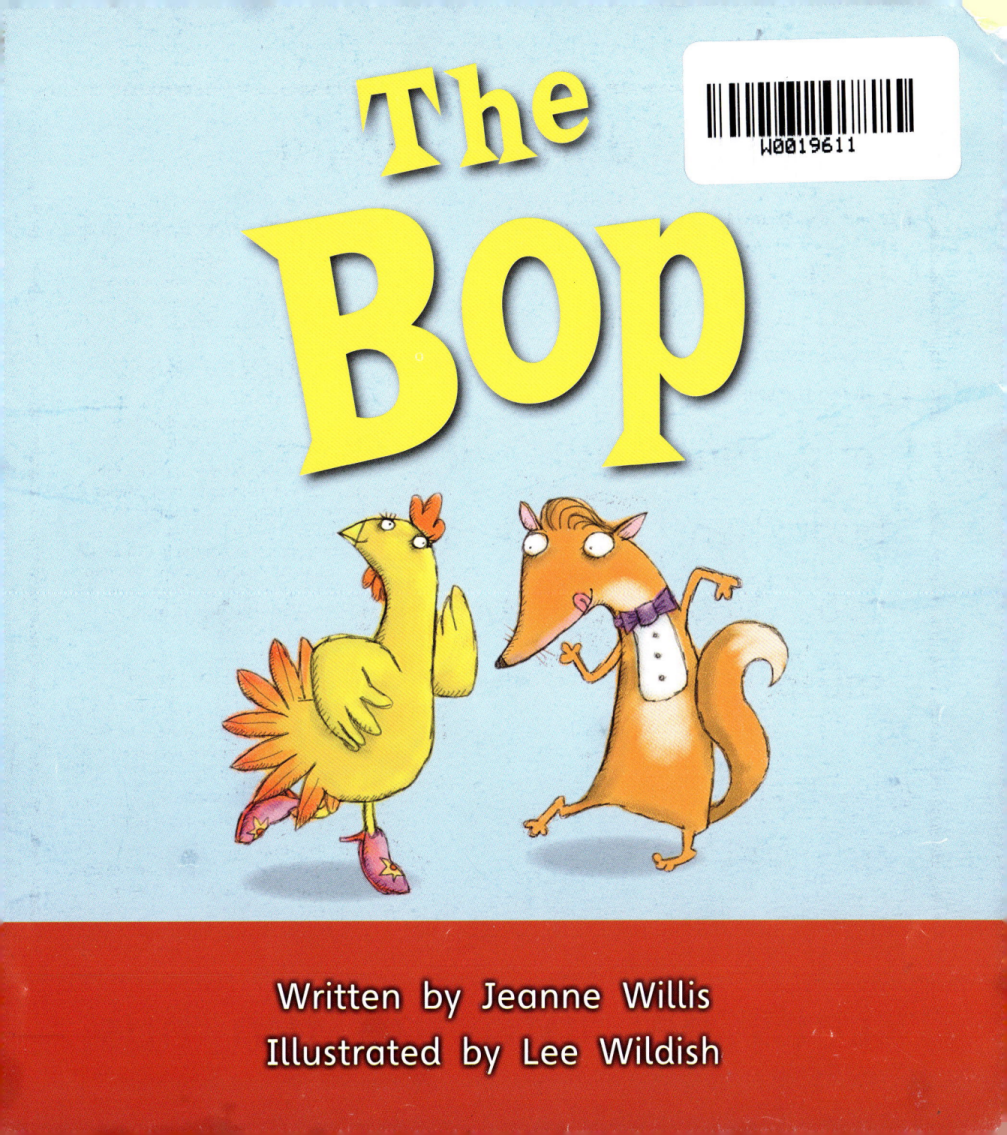

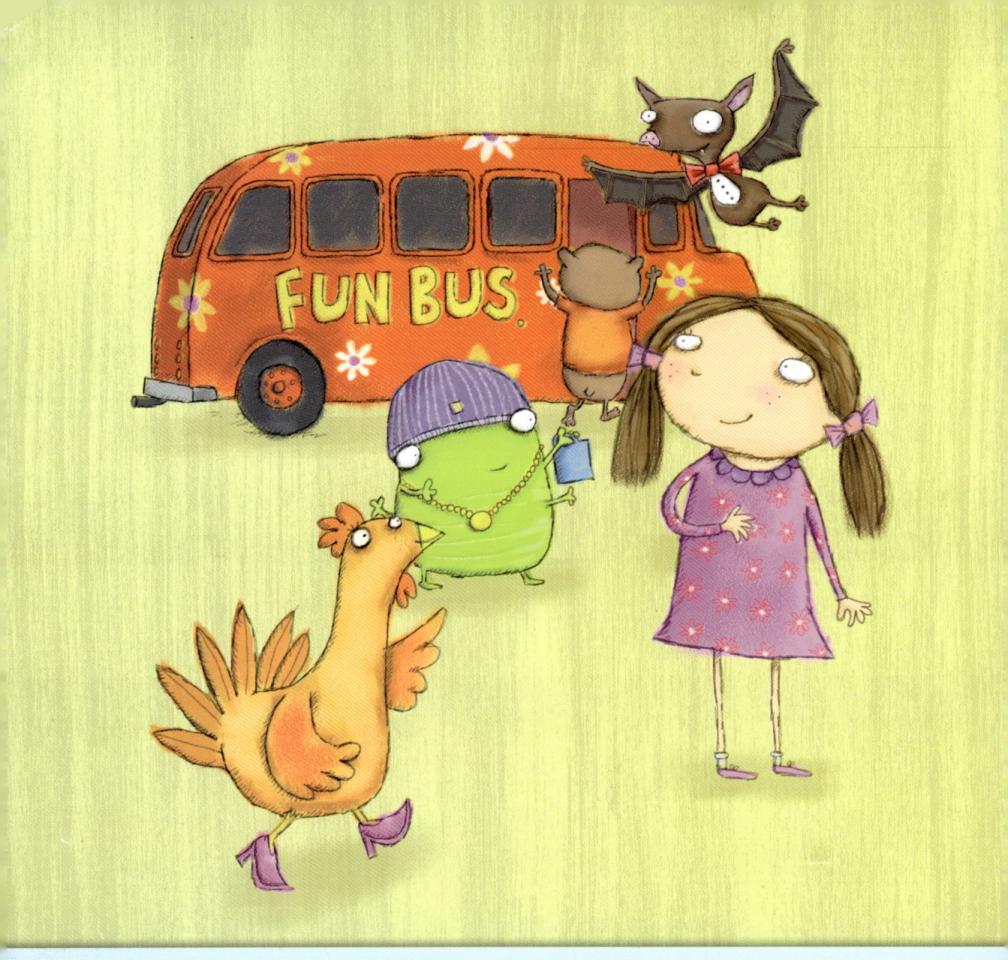

Let's get into the fun bus.

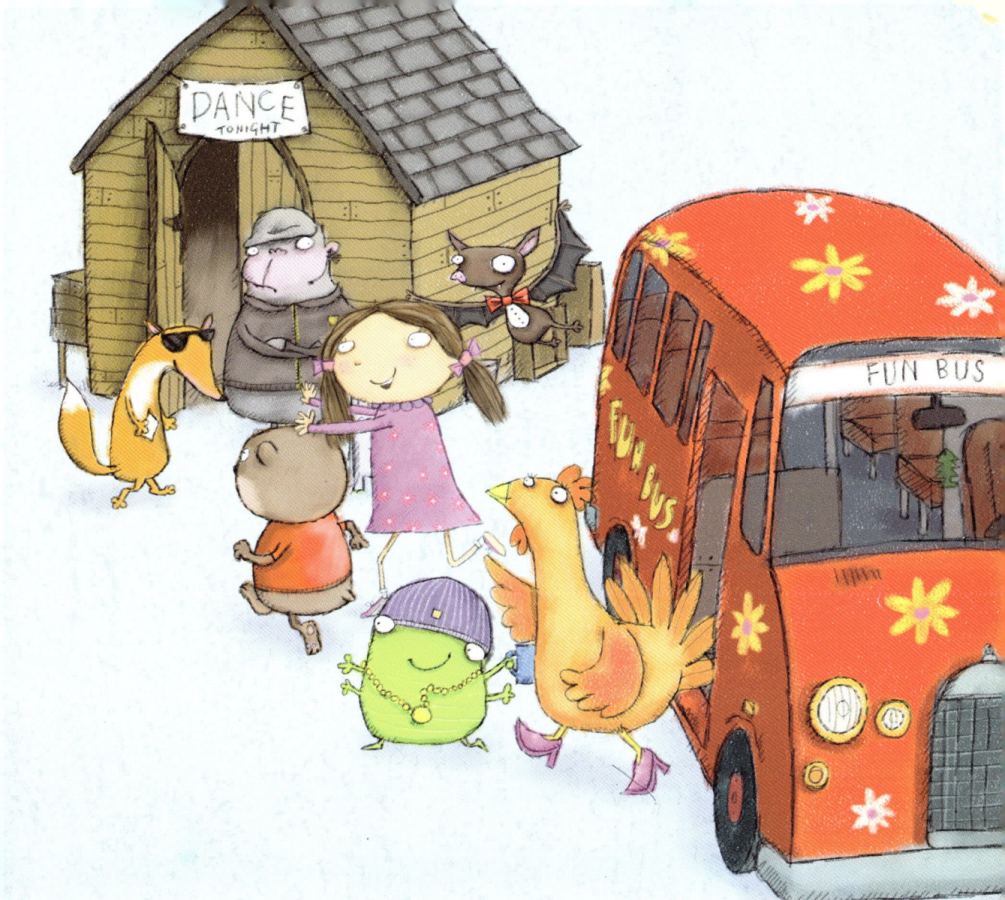

Go to the bop!

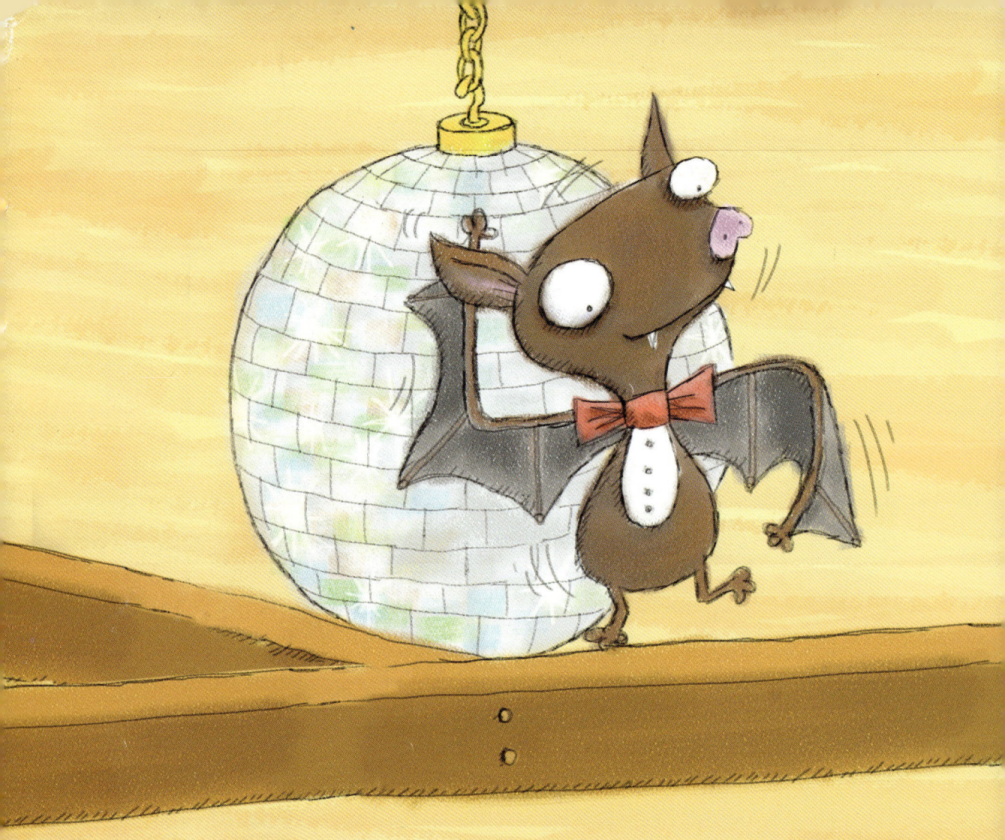

The bat can bob.
Bob, bob, bob!

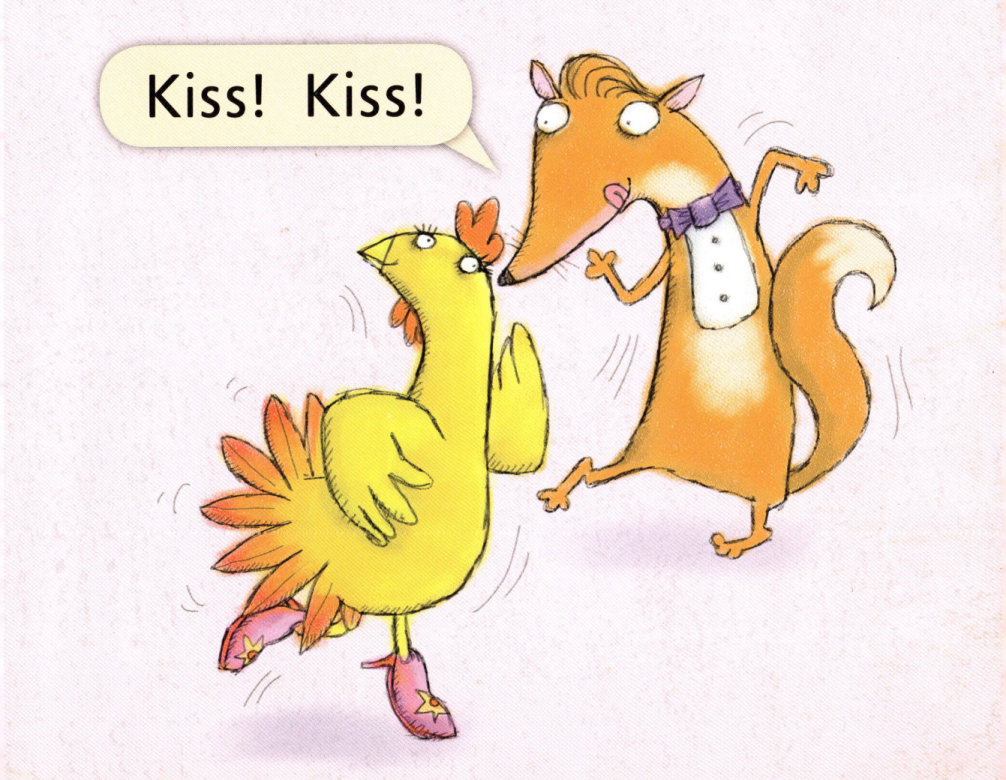

The hen can hop.
Hop, Hen, hop!

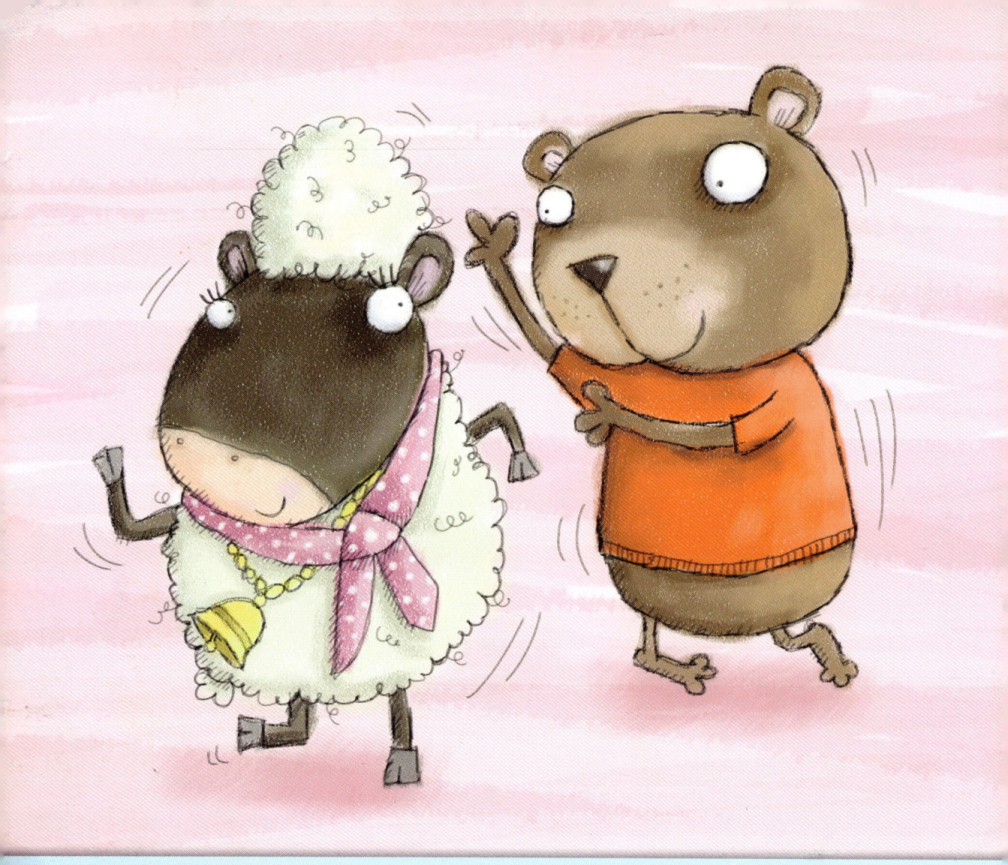

The cub can rock.
Rock it, Cub!

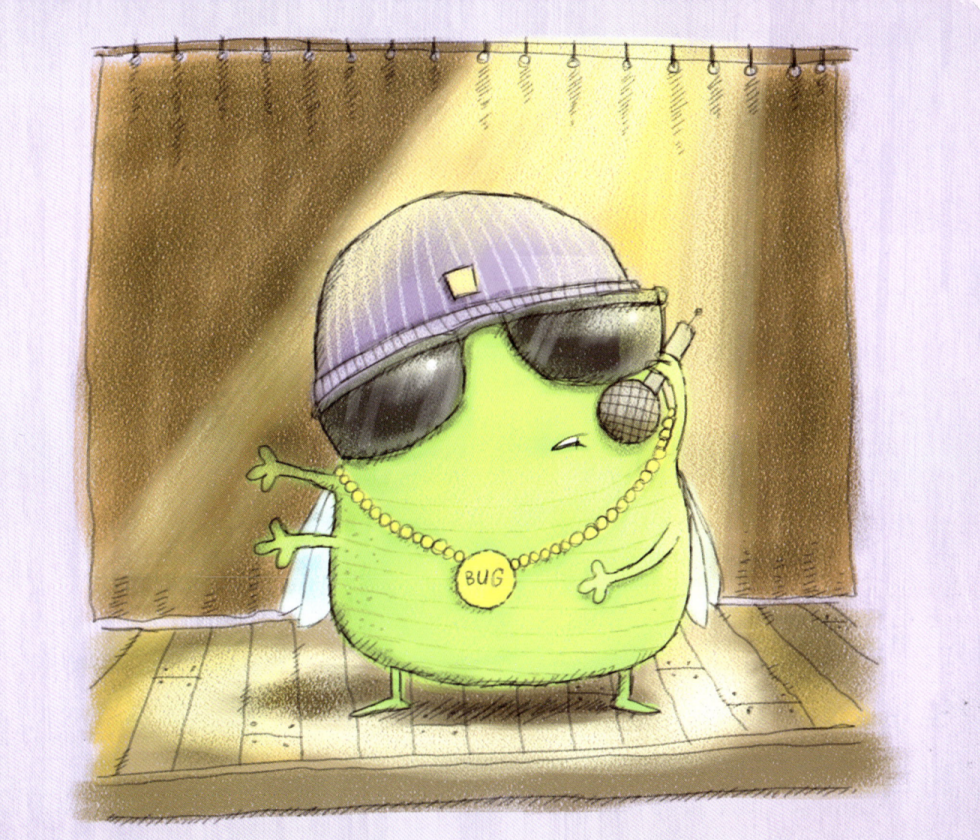

The bug can rap.
Rap, Bug, rap!

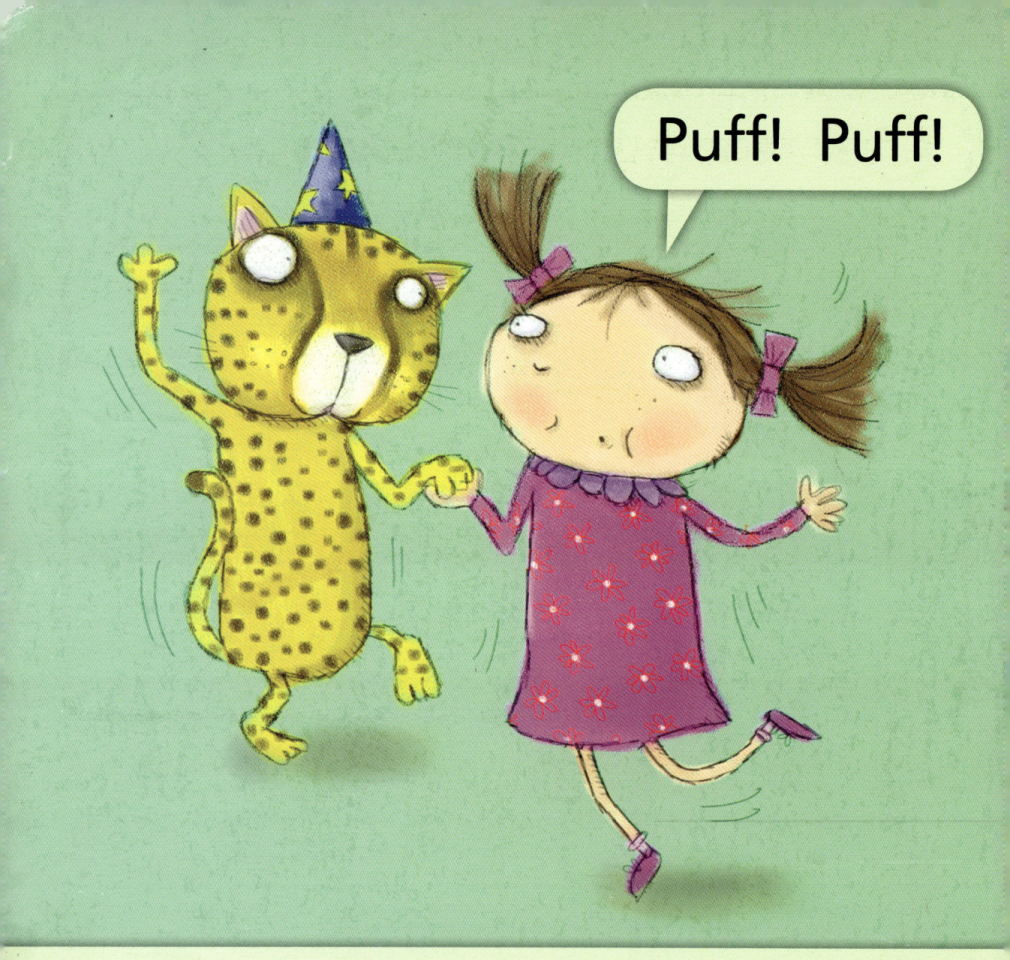

I can salsa!